Knucklehead poems

ALSO BY TONY KEITH JR.

How the Boogeyman Became a Poet

Knucklehead
poems
Tony Keith Jr.
Quill Tree Books
An Imprint of HarperCollinsPublishers

Quill Tree Books is an imprint of HarperCollins Publishers.

Knucklehead: Poems
Text copyright © 2025 by Anthony R. Keith Jr.
Illustrations copyright © 2025 by Julian Adon Alexander
All rights reserved. Printed in Harrisonburg, VA, United States of America.
No part of this book may be used or reproduced in any manner whatsoever without written permission except in the case of brief quotations embodied in critical articles and reviews. For information address HarperCollins Children's Books, a division of HarperCollins Publishers, 195 Broadway, New York, NY 10007.
www.epicreads.com

Library of Congress Control Number: 2024942797
ISBN 978-0-06-329605-3

Typography by David Curtis
24 25 26 27 28 LBC 5 4 3 2 1
First Edition

To Lil Chris.

May your beautiful thoughts become the words you write in poems.

Love,

Mr. Tony

Knucklehead
poems

DEAR KNUCKLEHEAD,

have you ever had a planet lodged in your belly
that could barely fit
because there is not enough free space for it
to expand into a land
with enough soil, seeds, water, sunlight, wind, and sand
to plant and produce vegetation for people as fresh as you?
as *cool* as you?
as laid-back as you are
while the world is spinning around counterclockwise
tryna birth itself into a language that breaks out of your body?

but you don't even blink, do you?
and you don't burp either,
because you know how blazing and catastrophic your breeze can be,
especially when something in the wind
is signaling that a storm is finna pull up
and twist your atmosphere around into too many pieces,
and you know that this will cause your roots to disconnect
at the exact point where they are tangled together the tightest.

and you know that your smoke and your haze
and your hail are astronomically powerful
whenever your calmed collectiveness
is shoved to the point of its mightiest.

. . . that's when your beautiful disaster
will spread across the atmosphere,
and your spirit will be unable to contain how wholesome you are,
and how complete, pulled together, and upright you appear
to a world afraid to recognize that the size of your body,
and the width, depth, girth, length,
and strength of your tongue
ain't things God made to threaten anyone.

and so, it is *their* fear, and their eyes, and their ears,
and their phobias, and their biases,
and their slick slurs, and their sneaky sneers
that have become words
that you and I are constantly translating
into a poetic love speech
that only we: us know how to fluidly speak.

it doesn't make any sense, Knucklehead,
that our celestial stature and our divine light
causes onlookers, bystanders, blabbermouths, naysayers,
law enforcement officers, laypersons, and lawmakers

to be afraid of what we might say,
or what we might do,
once we recognize that *their* problems with how *we* came out
with the world in us,
and with how we wanna show up,
as our full selves within it,
ain't got nothing to do with us: me: we: you.

and it doesn't help
that no one is explaining all that's going on to us
in a script that we can decode, interpret, and fully comprehend.
so we don't all call ourselves:
"ambitious," "inspirational," or "courageous,"
although we know that we're not:
"blasphemous," "ignorant," or "dangerous."

if anything, Knucklehead,
whatever force from whatever source
that created the planet that can't fit inside of you
is the same blast that brought about the one
rotating inside of me too.

so yeah,
I know what it's like to bite your tongue and taste salt
when letters, armed as weapons, are spoken to destroy you.
I know that what you really wanna say:

your arsenal, your defense mechanism,
ain't as sweet or as soft or as delicate as you are,
for real for real.
I know you be holding back too.

BECAUSE WORDS HAVE POWER.

letters are electrically charged, and when bonded together,
create enough energy to cause massive explosions.
words can blow tiny mountaintops into massive
    metaphorical erosions,
and it will be I, standing atop one of those mounds,
with words, syllables, phrases, vowels, and sounds,
and I'll be screaming:

"this is for all my brothas still dreaming!"

whose hue begins as black,
but you've been beaten down to blue.
who don't know who you are
because society has already defined you.
ain't got a pot to piss in, a window to throw it out of,
and no food to chew.
and so you're starving.

starving for knowledge,
not because you can't grasp the language,
but because no one took the time to teach you.
or claimed that you're too stubborn to listen,
or that your head is too thick to get a brick through.
or said you're nothing but a no-good,
pant-sagging, baby-making juvenile delinquent,
and that all you're capable of doing
is simply eating, sleeping, shitting, and screwing.

but brothas, I've got something different to tell you,
and as I do,
I invoke in myself the spirit of everything African within me:
from my forehead to my collarbone.
from my bloodstream to my skin tone.
from my strong back to my humble knees.
from my shinbone to my calloused feet.
and brothas, I declare you free!

no longer property.
no longer a weapon for society
to continue to arm you with
monstrous missiles of misguided perceptions of manhood
into your looking glasses.

so don't sleep while sitting in the back,
writing "RIP" for friends on that dirty desk.
instead dream about being in the front teaching those classes.
and stop being afraid to use slang.
I'm granting you the right to use the language of *your* people
to move the masses.
and don't wait in the back of the line to get to the front.
I'm giving you a lifetime supply of free VIP backstage passes!

and if someone says you didn't pay your way,
tell them, "it's already being deducted from my taxes!"
and if they say they need proof,
tell them they can find it printed on paper receipts,
made from trees, once used to whip enslaved Africans' backs.

and if they still got questions,
tell them they can call up the "Black Men's Headquarters"
and have them send transcripts through smoke signals
and Morse code dashes.
and if they still got questions,
tell them they can take a pin and prick your skin
and check your deoxyribonucleic acid,
better known as your DNA,
because they Don't Need Answers. they don't need anything.

and if they say they do,
tell them come see me, because I got you.
I'm holding y'all up on my shoulders giving you a higher view.
I'm breaking y'all through mountaintops
and wading through muddy waters,
and don't worry, because historically,
I've been known to split that shit in two.

so Knucklehead, if I gotta fight your battles
and if I gotta take your blows, trust that I will do it for you.
and I'll do it with a smile . . .
a smile as cool as the metaphors in the poems of Langston Hughes
and as pure as the vibrato in B. B. King's blues.
I'll do it while wearing a pair of black pants,
a black shirt, a black tie, some black socks,
and a cool-ass pair of black suede shoes,
and I'll be looking just like the rest of the men on the
  morning news,
but instead, I'll be screaming:

news flash! news flash!
Knuckleheads, America is trying to take your freedom,
but they can't take something that comes from within you.
they claim they got you by the balls,
but let's face it, you're a Black man,
and stereotypically, if they've got small hands,
they can barely grip one of your testicles.

so go ahead and tell them to step their game up,
take some vitamin C,
try eating some more fresh fruits and vegetables.

but no matter what they do, they will never be stronger than you.
we fight with one fist in the air,

but with me beside you, we can fight with the power of two.
so until you have gained the wisdom, Knucklehead,
and until you have learned how to work the system,
and until you can walk with your footsteps next to mine,
don't worry, I will carry you,
as long as you remember to pick up and carry those of us
left behind.

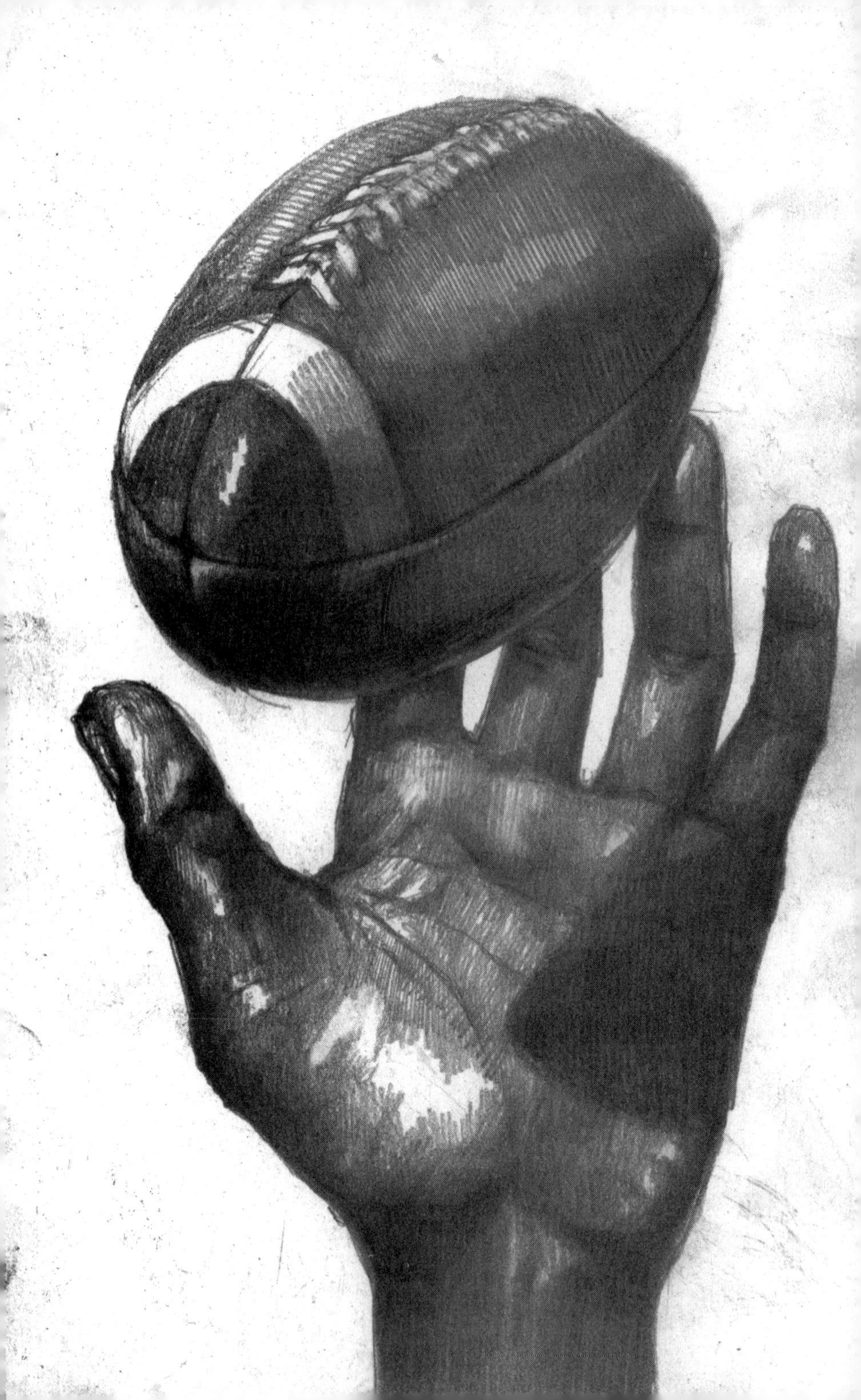

THE ONES STUCK IN SILENCE.

the ones stacked up behind bars,
backed into some black barricaded corner
with their chests flexed like brown puff adders,
as if swollen breath inflating tight bellies matter
when guarding limbs and protecting faces
and striking lightning before their thunder roars too soft
inside of hard spaces:

like prisons, where discovering safety and security
be like looking for mercy in masculinity,
be like searching for solace in captivity,
be like finding fortitude before freedom,
be like seeking faith without salvation,
be like asking God about love,
instead of praying about liberation,
be like clarity
when you're chained inside of a policed place,
where everyone has a human desire to be called by their name.
because being known as "inmate" and "number"
invite both blood and shame.

like playgrounds,
where I was never afraid to catch the ball,
I just hated what would happen if I didn't.
somebody would yell:

"butterfingers"
all of me:
a slippery Black boy too soft to catch and hold on to
masculinity:
hollow air wrapped in pigskin whirling toward my face,
which is the exact place where fists and salty stings from
sharp words
spoken by bullies who mastered the spiral and knew not to
fumble
would plant their punches, while I stumbled over myself
pretending to laugh when they pointed their fingers at me
and stabbed words into my soul like:

"punk"
all of me:
a brown-skinned ruffian
reduced to rendered fat from cow secretions,
churning hot and melting all over my flaming wrists
and my fingertips; flickering slick and shiny grease
that leaked all over my hands,
so I couldn't catch Black men's bravado

with enough precision to satisfy the sports team
who always picked me last
because I was a

"faggot"
all of me:
twigs torn from branches,
pulled apart from some thirsty tree.
stripped down to thin tips of dry wood
soaked in kerosene,
wrapped together in twine,
and craving for someone to light a match,
close their eyes,
and toss hot death in my direction,
where I stood like a

"pussy"
all of me:
an effeminate rebel.
a vagina colloquialism.
a metaphor for the sacred private place in Black women's
bodies
where all Black people are born.
a feral purring feline species
not to be confused with a

"bitch"
all of me:
a four-legged domesticated female K-9.
not a free human being,
not even a spirit capable of breathing,
not even a rhythmic heart worth beating.

truth is, Knucklehead, I preferred to grab flags tagged
around waists
after running from the huddle
rather than sprint headfirst into a stiff-armed tackle,
because for real for real,
I could be really unpredictable if a brawl began.

I FOUGHT LIKE NOBODY'S BUSINESS.

as if nary a person would've dared claim to have witnessed
my numerous failed attempts
at fleeing from the natural form in which I was born.
because being free like *that* ain't safe,
nor is it the norm.
which is why my arms flailed around in a circle
all frail and flimsy like *that.*
that's why I created a cipher of words
that whistled through a sharp lisp,
and balanced broken structures of masculinity
on the back-and-forth tip of my swollen limp wrists.

and that's why my limbs were a windmill,
spinning around whatever spiritual center
that also made my hips switch "a little too hard,"
especially when walking into a battle of wits
about gay boys and sword fights.
so, I was always all on guard and shit.
all cloaked in armor: my best outfit.

welded tight and shut in solid,
sealed up and suffocating underneath my brown skin:
all that melanin trying to survive on rhythm
without a place to dance,
except for that tiny space in between the palm of my hands,
where my fingers could perform circles around the wind,
and sway smoothly as if they were ceiling fans.

so yes, Knucklehead, I too have slapped back hard.
punched my power while trying to avoid feeling
what I really thought about myself:
short and simple
and way too nimble to hold my soul together:
all that flesh, loosely sticking meat to my
hollowed bones,
and spilling blood compressed deep down inside
the marrow,
leaking out any ounce of doubt
about my ability to be ferocious and feared
because when I was scared,
I swung to save cracks reflected in mirrors,
which are gifted with an ability to manifest transparency.
they can use a carbon copy of an image opposite its body
and fit, like a puzzle, all the pieces of us: whole.

and I'd stand there,
square foot in front of a shiny sheet made of aluminum and glass,
staring at X-rayed pictures of what I believed I looked like
when the whole world wasn't around to watch me
perform the parts of myself that wouldn't warrant questions
about my presence,
or my posturing amongst other people in public.

sometimes, I was ecstatic how my face showed up
and filled in that space between
how ugly I felt and how beautiful I am.
and so, I didn't blink before batting my eyelashes
and smiling back at myself in my body,
being myself in private,
practicing loving who I really was there   bare.

other times, I struggled to find evidence
that I appeared as clearly as I should.
my shoulders sloped too low and so,
my head couldn't support
all the pressure weighing down on my back,
which always reminded me that I wasn't really free.
so I just focused on some space between
my chest, the floor, and my feet.

IF ONLY I COULD'VE CARRIED THOSE BRICKS.

if only I didn't have to sacrifice the strength of my spine,
I would've built a wall big enough to withhold
some of the pressure that'd been building, boiling,
and bubbling up out of me from the inside,
because the weight was too heavy
and my spirit was too tired to pretend
that I didn't have the strength to bend over myself
before I was forced to break down,
before an upward smiling face became a busted backward frown,
before I would've walked barefoot on thorns and broken glass,
before I would've refused to run across a row of rusty nails
and tried not to laugh.

it required less energy to battle when I giggled,
when I suppressed the fighting words,
when I fidgeted and fiddled with my fingers
to avoid being the only tenor
in the middle of a swamp full of baritone singers.

but there wasn't nothing "funny" about me.
wasn't nothing tickling my flesh hard enough
to make me burst out in joyful hiccups.
wasn't nothing scratching at any of my itches.
wasn't nothing shaking any of the scabs loose from the skin
tied into my stitches.
I was the bag punched on the line of every joke in that comedy,
when for real for real, the pun was always in the words they
spoke about
how much they doubted me.

they ain't know I stored all my anger in a barrel
with a loose lid.
they ain't know I was a little too cautious and
a bit overprepared
for a gay Black kid.
they ain't know I was ready to say terrible things to people
when I permitted *my* insecurities to fight *their* battles,
when I decided to let *my* truth confront *their* egos.
when truthfully, I was afraid they would never let any
of *our* lies go.

I preferred not to be fluent in a language that told me who I
really was.
instead, Knucklehead, I chose to throw flames
with my tongue twisted in gasoline

and my heartbeat striking the match,
knowing that I could,
if I wanted to   blow it all.

BECAUSE WHEN I WRITE I'M DANGEROUS.

I be more lethal in pen than blurbs spoken out loud,
because written words are sharp.   they cut deep.
they be like daggers. they be like swords stuck in concrete.
they be like letters melted into stone.
them joints be spelling out loud all the hard shit I be tryna soften up
just enough to smoothly slice in between
all the rock and all the pebble,
and to sift through, and to split up all the shit,
and every single speck of sand and scared ideas I have
about losing my battle:

> my war with myself, my internalized civil unrest, my
> crusade for liberation,
> my freedom beating, breathing beneath my Black skin,
> digging up all my dirty roots and burning up all my sage,
> tryna clean up and straighten out all the stirred-up soil
> and all the smelly shit I be wanting covered forever.

a stench buried forever.
a rot swallowed into the earth.
a decay digested by gravity.
a corpse consumed in that space where the magma boils
like a bubbling pool of water on fire
in a place hot as hell, where I be cooking myself
in a simmering Crock-Pot full of all the salty, saucy, spicy, and
    sweet shit
I gotta deal with being burned alive by myself forever.

where I be a solitary flame.
where I be a Black crispy faggot on fire,
stuffed down there in the pit,
in the sink, where the kitchen and the baby's bathwater get lost,
'cause I be getting lost tryna discover myself
reflected in puddles of wonder I made from my own tears:

> a hoard of emotions liquefied from the heat
> caused by the anger rubbing on the inside of my veins:
>
> > an itch in my blood I could only scratch
> > with the blade I balanced between my tongue
> >   and the paper,
> > where my words carved holes in glass ceilings
> > inside of homes with stones scattered across
> >   the floor,

and where I made room for my escape from the
moments when
my fuel would meet my spark,
and I'd become a grenade
with the lynchpin attached by a thin layer of my Black skin,
and I'd be a bomb, ticking to the tune of my own time,
and so I'd make my own time to write.
I'd pause to extinguish myself,
to cool myself down,
to wash myself off,
to cleanse myself out.
to keep myself from turning into ashes.

and so I wrote,
to keep my gay Black ass far enough from the incinerator:
high above the point where my flesh would be scalding
on a cast-iron skillet disguised as a space for my safety,

and all I needed was some kind of saving words.

POETRY COMING TO THE RESCUE.

you can save someone from drowning,
and my daddy, who is a minister, says,
"son, if your sermon is good, you can save someone's soul."
well, I've never really been the kind of person to ask for help,
but if I needed some saving, trust me, you would know.
but I wouldn't be sending out an SOS message
or interrupting your regularly scheduled programs.
I wouldn't be sending it in an email, a text, a DM,
or posting anything on Facebook, TikTok, Snapchat, or Instagram.

instead, you'd find me on a stage.
usually, with a piece of paper in my left hand and a pen in my right.
my mouth would be wiiiiiiidddeeeee open and a vein poking out
of my neck.
my eyes would be shut tight as I focus on

[inhale] every [exhale]
[inhale] single [exhale]
[inhale] breath [exhale]

just to make sure that my lungs have enough capacity
to create words that defy the laws of gravity
and that swirl up into a vortex of knowledge,
causing supernatural catastrophes.
and while my poems ain't no tragedy,
there just might be some casualties
if you're not prepared to battle me.
but if you're feeling froggy, then JUMP!

'cause my poems are not for tricks,
and they certainly aren't for chumps.

I do *this* for a reason.

I write this for those of you with terminal diseases.
I write this for those of you who want to have sex,
but your parents are preachers.
I write this for those of you who want to learn,
but lack loving mentors and teachers.
I write this for those of you who love your mama,
but all she does is scream at ya.
I write this for those of you who love your daddy,
although his eyes have never seen ya.
I write this for those of you who miss getting a good night's sleep
after hearing your grandma sing a sweet song to ya.
I write this for those of you with negative energy,
and so like a magnet, bullshit just clings to ya.

I write *this* for you.

I write this for those of you whose sexuality is "unacceptable,"
until it receives some societal stamp of approval.
I write this for those of you who work so hard to create change,
you get frustrated, but you still maintain.
I write this for those of you who don't have answers,
yet one is always being forced from you.
I've learned that sometimes saying "I don't know" is a lie,
and that sometimes saying "I don't know" is the truth.
I write this for those of you who want to earn love,
but don't know that it's already been given to you.

I write *this* for you.

been battling poetry until my ink bleeds black and blue.
I'm just a superhero with a cape made of metaphors,
trying to use my words to simply save you.
. . . and yes, some of the words in my poems do rhyme,
but I've been doing it for a while, so it just happens sometimes.
and yes, memorizing a poem would make any performance good,
but if I could, I would pick up this book and read you my words,
just to make sure that my messages are never misunderstood.

I do *this* for a reason.

and this gift is not temporary,
it does not change with the seasons.
which means I can spit fire while the sky is hot,
or I can cool it down while the water is freezing.
and if "words having power" isn't something that you believe in,
then I can spit on my fingertips, reach out my palms,
and turn these written words on pages into a spoken altar call,
and I can start saving all of you heathens.

because I care about your futures. I care about your legacies.
I care about your destinies, and I want y'all to know my name.
I want y'all to look up in the sky and scream out:
"is that a bird? is that a plane?"

and I'll be flying by, shouting, "no, it is poetry, and I'm a poet."
a social agent of change.
piecing letters to words and words to sentences,
and sentences to sounds.
I can leap over metaphors with a single bound.
I am powerful enough to spark protests for equality in ghetto
communities,
talk slicker than silly politicians
creating policies that grant rich folks immunities.

see, I didn't choose to be saved by poetry;
poetry chose me.

poetry crept up inside my mama's womb
and poetry started tickling me.
I've been speaking in rhythmic patterns since I was in grade three.
I'll just continue until I'm through.

so, who am I?

well, I'm just a simple superhero with a cape made of metaphors,
trying to use my words to save *you.*

DEAR KNUCKLEHEAD,

perhaps you are like me:

always figuring out if your soul and your skin
are thick enough to protect your body from sticky stones
thrown from the mouths of those who know
that spoken words have the power to spit out freedom
and break in bones.

and if perhaps you are like me,
then you too wanna be in the light every day,

be a light every day too

be a light every day to people also tired of existing
in darkness.

so you must also know how to muster up
more than enough of yourself
to force a beam to burst from your tongue
as bright as your life can command
just so the world will understand
that, in fact, you are not silent and invisible.
you are instead an invincible mirror facing the solar system:

an infinite black space where the history of who you are
dances in the eye of every single night sky
and on the tiptoes of every single twinkling star:
the ones that burn bright holes into a galaxy
that for some people might seem a bit too far.

but if perhaps you are like me,
then you too believe that distance is only just a matter of the heart,
and that for us to *really* glow as gigantic and as galactic
as we know we are,
then love absolutely, unequivocally, has to be the biggest part.

and if perhaps you are like me,
then you also know how to prevent yourself
from falling apart into scattered pieces.
as for me, it's always been poetry protecting my peace.
and each piece I write and read to myself on
the inside and out loud,
in the mirror, in the shower, under my breath,
on the microphone,
at the open mic, at the poetry slam, in the cipher,
in the schools,
at the juvies, at the libraries, at the museums, on the sidewalks,
on the subway, for my grandmother, for my friends,
for my man,
all of them add fuel to keep my fire alive,

so that the universe can hear my response to its call,
confirming that I am indeed still flaming and fighting.

. . . still battling with Boogeymen in my dreams and in my writing
because Black boys, all of us, still out here
grinding for our time, waging war for our moment,
hustling for our present, praying for our future,
hoping for centuries that we can finally smile, and sing,
and imagine,
and wonder, and play, and relax, and prepare,
and learn, and believe, and think, and hug,
and perform our poems without being punished.

A ZERO-PENALTY OPPORTUNITY.

like that squad of brown-skinned boys I saw riding bikes
down busy blocks between 23rd & P, NW, DC,
owning streets, on two wheels, in two lanes,
pedaling too fast to notice
drivers honking, pedestrians cussing, and potholes ahead.
instead, they were acrobats in flight,
half in the air, half on the ground,
tumbling around asphalt concrete and southern winds.

I hope they saw my smile
and heard my applause at the freedom on their faces,
while I watched in awe,
those lil Knuckleheads looking like me: free.
sliding through traffic, ignoring the law
as if all lights are green forever.
as if all their tires will tread tight forever.
as if the red, white, and blue squealing sirens behind them
meant their bodies could coast cool forever.

AND THAT AIN'T THE CASE.

it certainly wasn't for Mike, Eric, Tamir, Gary & nem:
Black boys killed in a correlation between how America treats
money
and how it treats its people
like cash, coins, bills, and bodies,
all commodities, meant to be traded in exchange
for products, goods, and services.
the denomination depends on the purpose,
but a lot of us don't know what our purpose is,
so, all we do is consume, rarely do we create.
the result is our wealth has become a loan with a high interest rate,
and somehow, we've defaulted.
it appears our payments arrived a little too late.

granted, we have our checks and balances,
but let's be honest, none of our checkbooks are really balanced.
we need to check our balance.
check to determine what the status of our
account is.

because the last time I checked, we were deeply in the red,
although we used to be in the Black.
now, blood-covered brown men, hands up, holes in their backs.

racism is making withdrawals,
depleting our reserves, depriving us of the positives.
choosing when to spend or to save Black lives
has become a government prerogative.
and none of these statements make any sense:
        at least six shots and zero arrests,
        except for those engaging in peaceful protest.
either the math is corrupt or our thick, scary skin isn't so tough,
especially when a bullet is going in.

and if this is a game, there's a flawed strategy to win.
and if this is a gamble, then I'm not willing to bluff,
because betting on Black bodies means we're risking too much,
and we've already lost enough.

we break, but we're not even.
our chips aren't stacked up, nor are they increasing.
we're trying to keep count of our kings,
but we're penalized for cheating.
where is our credit because these scores are deceiving.

our treasures are falling through holes in our pockets,

and we can't reach in to save them, or else cops will try to stop it,
using tear gas to block it, so all our change falls to the ground.
then pigs break our banks with 9mm rounds,
and all our currency melts in the streets, transaction complete,
don't ask for any receipts.
here's an open letter to [insert the town] police,
I represent a collection agency and you owe us a debt.
our demand is that you supply us with justice,
and this ain't no wolf-ticketed threat.
your integrity has been compromised because we ain't been
paid yet.
and until we are, here is what you can expect:

1. our feet will pound on pavements until you make full payment.
2. we will charge with our voices
until there's some charges on those invoices.
3. we will mobilize and protect every asset we have left,
even if you call us "looters" or claim it is "theft."
4. we will be persistent; apathy has no place in this movement.
5. we will publish our own narratives;
we don't need Fox or CNN to do it.
6. we will express rage; anger is a necessary stage.
7. we will not rest until there's an arrest.
8. we will love ourselves.
9. we will love you.
10. your payment is past due.

I DON'T HAVE TO IMAGINE BEING BLACK.

being brilliant and misunderstood by the same people
who only seem to understand you after you've exfoliated.
. . . after you've scraped yourself down to the white meat
to expose that layer of skin where color and soul meet.
where my ancestors,
whose tongues were split, pitchforked, and code-switched,
learned to spit and speak, and sing, and scream,
and stand on stages while the world bet and bid and bargained
and debated about their ebony brain,
and their Black boisterous bodies,
and centuries later, I'm questioning my value,
askin if speakin like dis is e'en worf it?

I know what it's like to *not* know what words mean.
I know what it's like to have letters chained together on paper,
locked up, heavy, just sitting there still and silent, not moving.
I know what it's like to carry the burden of words on your back.
to bow to prevent your bones from breaking beneath them.

but I also know what it's like to *know* what words mean.
I know what it's like to have letters breakdance on blue lines
that look like horizontal skies cutting through white space.
I know what it's like when words fly off the page
and land on your face.

I know what it's like when words look like you
because I'm a descendant of enslaved Africans:
a people, separated by their tongues on plantations, on purpose.
a people who published translations about their liberation
through poems and songs on purpose.
a people who prayed and protested, and protected
all the parts of Black speech they couldn't speak in public,
but they spoke in private through the spoken word on purpose.

there is a purpose to this poem.

so, white people,
please stop telling me how your great-great-great-grandparents
are Polish, and Irish, and Italian,
'cause it comes from a place of privilege,
and I don't know what place . . .
I don't know what village of Mother Africa your ancestors might've pillaged.

what great-great-great price they paid
for my great-great-great-grandparents on that auction stage,
but I do know that I come from people
who persisted while they were being purchased, on purpose.

there's a purpose to this poem.
dis poem is an apology for e'ry beautiful Black verb
I tried to camouflage in white words.
for e'ry moment of my bein,
when I ain't know who I was bein,
'cause bein Black meant dat I was worth more den
da White worlds dat I be in.
an bein as tho I'm a human bein
with a tongue trapped in a cage it ain't ask to be in.
historically, it was beat in,
but da beat in my ancestors' bones
made sure I kept dis "be" in,

so, dis poem den is an apology.
for da intellectual abuse dat began in my youf.
my ancestors would say: but look at you
standin on stages like we taught you.
flippin, foldin, balancing, and beamin
two different languages in da air:
da American Standard and Black savior faire.
sho is impressive. sho is polished.

sho is distinguished. sho is debonair.
but to capture its essence just in writing ain't fair;
you need an audience there:
a sanctuary of people willing to watch you wrestle
and reconcile wif ya self and your words
and to produce a publication so worthy of praise,
it deserves a round of applause,

and I propose dat I am *the* purpose of dis poem.

I THINK SOME WHITE FOLKS BE CRUSHING ON ME.

not like prepubescent imaginations of love,
more like romanticized moments of Black voyeurism,
'cause they like looking at me and stuff.
always complimenting my style and my speech and my smile.
like they want to copy my speech and copy my style.
and I always smile at them, 'cause they're always smiling at me,
but we are reflections in an eclipsed mirror:
their shadow over my shine,
so, we both don't see how uncomfortable we are
with the fact that I am brilliant.

we're always fascinated by how well I can articulate my thoughts,
and how well my words can pick apart sound waves and shit
with my sexy, slick, sharp, smart tongue.

sometimes I think they wanna kiss me inside of my mouth.
sometimes I think they wanna taste what I'm saying,
'cause I speak in sweet and sour.

and we wonder why our words differ in power;
it's because we differ in power.
somehow, my volume always appears bolder, bigger, Blacker, louder.

and it's always an awkward performance of avoidance.
some intentional disregard of the obvious.
so, we just dance on broken jewelry boxes,
spinning around the fact that our rhythms just ain't the same
and we both know it.

we both know my step is a little cooler,
and that I stride a little smoother in my Black genes,
that I am brown skin matching Black beats,
that I am choreographed stitches at my seams.
I look good and stuff.

and we smile at my anomaly:
my elephant amongst whales:
my gigantism in infinite space:
my fortitude and my frail:
my wax and my wane.
because the same Blackness that captivates them
is the same Blackness that keeps me captive just the same.

I've got an angel on my shoulders telling me to love myself.
and I got a demon saying, "be quiet."

I've got an angel saying, "speak the truth."
and I got a demon saying, "stay silent."

I've got an angel saying, "the world is listening."
and I got a demon saying, "keep that stuff private."

but this truth can't contain itself because historically,
people like me spark riots.
people like me curate chaos.
people like me add fuel to fiery lips
and spark flames to burning tongues.

so white people, I'm sorry,
but I hope you don't think that your flattery
will somehow tame my capacity
to be one of the dangerous ones.
because there's a protest taking place in the back of my throat
and a movement marching from the roof of my mouth
that's carrying voices of Black folks from DC's southeast
Alabama Avenue
all the way to the state of Alabama's Deep South.

and this gift is not for your entertainment.
it is not to make you comfortable with your skin.
shoot, I'll treat open mics like civil rights countertop sit-ins.
which means I ain't moving, I ain't waiting, I ain't accommodating,

I ain't tolerating, I ain't assimilating.

for real for real, Knucklehead,
I be strategically agitating and infiltrating
while they just think that I'm fascinating.

DEAR KNUCKLEHEAD,

you know how sometimes everything seems impossible,
and people be tryna convince you otherwise?
they be speaking worldly old words of wisdom like:
"it'll be okay, baby," "have faith," "sky's the limit,"
"there are reasons and seasons for such and such,"
and "God don't make any mistakes about this and that."

and they be saying all this while rubbing a small hole
in your back,
right in the spot where your dreams first got stuck.
back when someone clipped the feathers from your wings.
back when they lied to you about some fictitious permanent
barrier
that's s'posed to exist at the exact altitude where your
dreams
are flying amongst a multitude of floating monsters:
every single one of them pretending to be
guardians of the truth.

gladiators fighting for their honor in an arena
full of fibs about you.
and everyone is cheering for them to win.

and so now, the thought of being two feet above the ground
or walking with both feet way up in the clouds
doesn't bring the warm and fuzzy feelings they said would come
about.

instead, all of it scares the absolute shit out of you?
makes your stomach gurgle, don't it?
makes your throat dry out?
makes your lungs collapse?
makes you heavy up front
and so you fall face forward over yourself
and right back into a cycle of believing
that whatever it is you desire from the world
ain't worf having belief in?
and so it's easier, cheaper, safer, better, quicker,
and more convenient
for you to pack up your purpose's bag and tell It to be leaving.

it sucks, don't it?
waiting on the thing you know is yours,
but the universe wanna try to see if your skin will ungather itself
near the tip of your anxiety, the zenith of your Zen,

the apex of your worry, the vortex of your patience,
all before you fold in on yourself and squish the very thing
that you've been hard-pressed to feel for so damn long.

it's hard, ain't it?
breathing in air that won't fill your lungs with enough volume
to shout out high enough to hear your ancestors' echoing voices:
the ones you accidentally silence out as simply white
noises.
and the whole time,
they already knew you'd forget what they said
and so you've never read
the messages they left for you
inside of the droplets drying on the morning dew.

ain't anxious about the waiting too?
the in-between time when you're s'posed to just sit there
and anticipate when God is gonna do the thing that God does
whenever you know there's more for you out there beyond the stars:
that space you're scared to be in because being way up
there
is too far from where you are
and absolutely where you want to go.

so what else can you do
but think about the amount of time passing by

all while remaining in pursuit of the very thing you've been chasing
since the day your wildest ideas became real-life moments
that reminded you why you are here,
and what you're supposed to be doing
with all the energy that you brought into the world
on the day you were born?

and if you are like me (with all your words and whatnot),
saying all the things you can't speak out loud:
which don't really matter,
because the speaker in your head has a clearer microphone:
a crystal picture of your voice reflected in the
mirror.
then you, too, are tryna make sense of all this ambivalence
about the inevitable moment when your dreams will land in
your hands,
and God won't laugh but will say,
"okay, here they are, Knucklehead, now go forth with your plans."

IF YOU FAIL TO PLAN, THEN PLAN TO FAIL.

at least that's what my daddy says.
and my daddy loved the bottle more than he loved the mirror.
he drank firewater until his voice boiled over
and his tongue became bitter.

and I look just like my daddy,
and I'm scared as shit because I want a kid who looks just like
me too:
a brilliant little youngin who is not desperate in their attempt
to stitch together an inkwell for a father:
a blueprint, a literal "writes of passage,"
something to remedy the moment that would disrupt their wonder
if God was ever more than just a Bible tale.

because God meant something to me:
a brilliant gay little Black boy
whose daddy thought he could talk to God
if he could just get high enough.

but my daddy could never get high enough.
he couldn't stay afloat
on Jack, Coke, and a crooked smile.
my daddy found false repentance in the smoke
and in the clouds.

I was a brilliant gay little Black boy
who built a wall of rhythmic stories
and wrapped them around my skin,
who learned to walk through the world wearing camouflage,
making it easier to pretend that my "girl-friends" were my
"girlfriends."

I knew how to hide in the color and the curiosity
about the boys and my heartbeat,
which had nothing to do with my absent addicted father,
which had nothing to do with my beautiful benevolent Black
mother:
a wonder woman who questioned her capacity to teach
manhood
to a son who hid truths in his metaphors,
who etched secrets onto his bones,
who tattooed nightmares on skeletons that he kept quiet
inside of the closet.

but Knucklehead, I don't perform in a cocoon anymore.

now my words have wings,
and now I can fly through the smoke and in the clouds
and with my dreams.
and just like my daddy *used* to do, I get high.

I CALL HIM "POP" OUTSIDE OF THE POEMS.

Pop would take me and my sister as kids to see fireworks
on the Fourth of July.
us, bonded together like sunrise and sunset,
would anticipate the transformation of the sky.
terrified of the POW, POP, and CRACKLE,
our hearts would rhythmically skip beats,
and we'd sound like two left feet
trying to tap-dance in sync.

us: we, cautious and curious children,
pictured loud colors exploding on black canvas
while holding Pop's hands:
me, on the side of his heart,
and she, somewhere near his liver.
he'd swing us with his elephant trunk arms
as if playing organ keys,
fluidly changing chords in between each and every step.

we'd eat strawberry licorice that looked like thin pink shoelaces
and we guzzled down red bubbly Rock Creek's Tahitian Treat
as if moon-bathing on an urban beach.
concrete felt like sand beneath our sneaks.

looking up at God,
we'd hold our breath and secure our spirits in place
while watching crackling fire fly high,
aiming at somewhere in space.

POW! CRACKLE! POP!

looked like golden palm trees up there.
like the sky was chewing crayons.
like a rainbow forgot it was nighttime
and managed to leave pieces of itself behind.
like squeezing life out of a dead dream.

sometimes I'd want to ask Pop if fireworks dyed the clouds
or if they scared the birds.
wasn't sure if birds could fly at night.
especially with all that ruckus,
there was never a single wing of freedom in sight.

I thought maybe if I closed my eyes,
the darkness wouldn't shine so bright.
and that when I opened them,

I could transform myself into the light,
and that I could get closer to the POW! CRACKLE! POP!

that I could get closer to Pop:
a Biblical man who, to this day, reminds me about eyes not seeing,
about ears not hearing,
about folks whose hearts may never encounter
all that God's got in store for me.

AS IF IT WERE THAT EASY.

ain't no passports to stamp when traveling
light-years and sound waves after your purpose.
you just gotta remain vigilant when crossing trivial territories
where the landscape, all broken and ragged
and dry and cracked,
will try to convince your feet
that walking all that way won't be worth the prize.
and that if you try to float barefoot and blindfolded above ground,
gravity will call your bluff
and suck you back down into the center of chaos.

and it ain't easy tryna protect your peace,
which can be like:
creating spiritual conditions around the cellular walls of your flesh
that are thick enough
to wrap around the pierced and punctured parts of yourself
that you prefer to pretend aren't perfect.

it can be like:
concrete words from affirmations that have softened, stirred up,

and constricted themselves at your core,
suffocating you with knowledge about
why you *really* don't hate to love yourself
as much as you say so, inside and out loud.

plus, it don't help
that all the bullshit Black folks be hearing about ourselves:
creatures in the trenches, rats in the gutter, spiders in a trap,
and the main problem with policy, police reports, scriptures,
jokes, statistics, and rumors are on full blast, in full press.
all of that mess
be stampeding and trampling
and pussyfooting around on the tip of our tongues
for what feels like an eternity.

so we can't say it . . .
and so we can't see all the pink elephants
performing cartwheels on curved ceilings
while wearing rose-colored glasses.

and so we won't say it . . .
and so we can't smell the confidence
crammed at the crux of our subconscious:
the mass of greatness
situated somewhere at some point in our lives
when we began to hoard away

every single reason we've heard for why we can't be great
when the universe comes to test us:

some destined point in time when God will show up
to check our birthmarks,
to search inside the sounds of our voices
to make sure our skin and our songs are petrified enough
to ward off and sustain
all imminent and potential threats made by predators of our
purpose:
people spiteful of our steps,
folks eager to encroach upon our front line,
sniffing, listening, prancing around that point where
they know
we're too afraid to admit the possibility that we'll forget
our mission,
fall out of line, stray from our paths,
wander back to the plantation,
trade in knowledge of self for a discount on mental
hibernation.

BUT YOU WON'T CATCH ME SLEEPING.

not while it's raining, while it's pouring,
while a whole lotta people still snoring,
while I'm watching them yawning,
waiting for the crack of dawn and
trying to get the rooster before it crows and
generating ink in my pen to start flowing,
so I can wake them up with *this* poem.

and I'm going to scream it loud
like an annoying alarm clock that won't snooze.
bang into their frontal lobe
like the morning after a long night with cheap booze.
hmpf, look at some of those fools
peacefully sleeping on their goose down pillows,
Egyptian cotton sheets, and chic chenille throws,
but little do they know, the child that made them
has an empty belly with no toilet bowl
and can barely get any sleep,
trying to make a pillow out of their elbows.

but why would they know?
that's because they're busy sleeping.
they're full from consuming reality TV shows that Americans
idolize
one-dimensional, egotistical, broken individuals
who ain't got the cash to count all their *g*'s.
nor the common sense to look above their heads
and count some of those *z*'s.
shoot, where I come from,
you got kids enrolled in pocketbook broke public schools,
who can flow better than most of them fools
simply by reciting their ABCs.

so, can we please get them some textbooks
that weren't made in the '80s?
can we please give them a curriculum that teaches them
that not all their ancestors were enslaved?
that getting whipped and picking cotton was not all they did.
we gotta get back to the basics.
ancient Africans ain't need laptops to build pyramids.

and although the Black history taught to me
suggested we were never free,
I simply won't buy it.
so, thank you, Mr. Lincoln, for writing it,
but my freedom never required your emancipation.

my ancestors already wore crowns, birthed communities
and were queens and kings of a zillion nations.
so, you can't give me back something
that was never yours for the taking.
          let alone yours for the keeping.

but Knucklehead,
people can't escape bondage while they're still sleeping.
they can't escape the stereotypes and lies seeping,
and the poison pumping into their bloodstream
that's controlling their breathing.
got them afraid of waking up,
'cause when they do,
America will squeeze their lungs tighter
and put them right back to sleep again.

but they can go ahead and rock a bye to whatever lullabies
while I keep my feet moving.
I'll be busy tracking down the Sandman
while some of them are busy snoozing.
and when I catch him, I'm gonna tell him:
hey, Sandman, stop tryna sprinkle us into being
sweet sleeping residents of Dreamland.
in fact, you can take your rent check from the political puppets
who be out there prancing on the world's stage.

because my *people* been had good credit.
    shoot, ain't we the ones who should be getting repaid?

nah, you'll never find me sleeping.
I'll keep one eye open while guarding my sheep
and if their nightmares get too close to home,
I'll wake them up simply by reciting this poem.
and I ain't afraid because even Dr. Martin Luther King Jr.
was trained in "poets speak,"
and so, the slurs of my words will sound like an inaugural speech.

and I'm electing every one of my ancestors to cabinet seats:
appointing Rosa Parks as the Secretary of Transportation,
appointing Dr. Edward Alexander Bouchet as the Secretary of
  Education,
appointing Garrett Morgan as the Secretary of Energy,
and I'll dig deep down in my roots and appoint Harriet Tubman
    as the Secretary of Homeland Security.

so, don't sleep, Knucklehead,
we've been doing this for centuries.
don't let the past, present, and future state of this nation
force you into a state of mental hibernation.
you have the right to be awakened.
you have a right to make decisions.

you have a voice at the table.
you need not ever ask for permission.

so wake up and stretch your arms out WIIIIDDEEEE with me.
yaaawwwwnnn and let your morning breath reek of democracy,
wipe the crust of bondage from your eyes.
remember your dreams and forget the lies.

IT'D BE A BRAND-NEW DAY.

there'd be no more long shadows cast on windows.
no more cold nights in spring.
no more floods in the valleys, darkness in alleys,
because now the caged bird would sing.

there'd be no more nightmares overnight, anywhere.
only dreams come true.
clouds will have passed and sunshine will last.
and gray skies would now be blue.

there'd be no more dusty floors.
there'd be no more squeaky doors.
there'd only be whispers heard in the wind.
there'd be no more sadness, only wishful gladness.
no more, because a brand-new day begins.

there'd be no more agonizing pain, no more frozen rains.
there'd only be tears cried of joy.
there'd be no more frustration, in any duration.
for Knucklehead, *this man*, he was a boy.

and it'd be all over, the gloom that hovered.
and there'd be nothing to do but smile.
and you could be smelling seashells,
dropping pennies in wishing wells,
and watching the stars, saying, "ohhhh look at how they fly."

BUT IT'S TOUGH WAITING FOR MORNING.

I be in bed sometimes way past midnight and well before dawn.
with my back flat, face up, hands tucked, pupils stuck.

I be staring at the ceiling while the clock be ticking
and the seconds be ringing.
and minutes be singing.
I swear I be spending hours wishing I was sleeping.

sometimes I can't stop thinking about the moment between
being awake and dreaming.
sometimes I can't stop listening to my heart beating.
sometimes I can't stop scratching the itch tingling on my eyelids,
and the buzzing flying around my knee.

all that anxious energy got my stomach tap-dancing,
bouncing to the beat of my barely shallow breathing.

I be contemplating why I be writing poems in my head,
wondering how long I'll be featuring them

on the stage of my open mind mics,
            praying it won't be like that every evening.

I don't think I wear eyeglasses in my dreams though.
I figure, if I'm unconscious, my vision must be crystal clear.
so there'd be no need to squint tight to let in sunlight.
no lenses to wipe clean enough to perceive distances far or near.
wouldn't have to worry about wire cracks in frames
or if my temple tips were too tight,
or whether the bridge, broken, might bend off the hinge.
wouldn't be a need to be concerned about my sight.

wouldn't need a prescription preventing me from focusing.
no medication would need to be applied to my pupils
to heal how I fixate on noticing how I look high flying, finding
    fortune,
finishing first, freedom fighting, and falling in love.

I

DEAR KNUCKLEHEAD,

it's interesting, "love," ain't it?
a feeling, an action, a word, a language, God.
all the underlined patterns of the universe glued at the edges of
four letters.
and I don't know about you, but whenever I see L, O, V, and E
standing next to each other on the same line like that on purpose—
for reasons that expand beyond the definition of their
linguistic union,
or whatever symbolic interaction that occurred when
they first met,
which I guess is when they decided to form lyrics
that became poems
about people who desire to be *with* other people
for joy, for excitement,
for companionship, for pleasure, for protection—
I pause to notice their placement amongst a string of other
I's (eyes) and *u*'s (yous):
us: we: the ones holding "love" on the outside, or somewhere in
the middle,

upright and toward the center, smack-dab right in the heart,
which is interesting because love is never described
as a real vital organ,
it is never our blood-pumping rhythmic beating body part.

no, love is always made from the
upside-down red triangle with a dent in its core.
and we proudly display love across our chest,
on our sleeves, on our faces.
we wear love as a sticky symbol embroidered
in decals stuck on our windows
and wrapped in the greetings we give
and get, or not, on the 14th of every February.
love, I think,
comes from some ancient holy tongue, cheek, and spit
situation.
some supernatural script that ain't written down,
but can be spoken by anybody.
a saintly dialect created during the eon God
spent developing our "chemistry."
back when God was conducting experiments about humanity,
back when God was answering questions about the stuff that
joins people, all of us,
together somewhere at the subatomic level.

I imagine that kind of research required God
to endure a great deal of trial and error.

I bet God had no choice but to test methods
    that hadn't existed before.
I bet God jigsawed puzzle pieces and
    repurposed private parts of people
and put them in glass beakers full of brilliant ideas.
I bet God bounced them: us: we back and
    forth hoping that whatever bonded together
would become something everyone
    everywhere could understand,
and would be able to recognize when it: love:
    God: us: we smiled at them on the paper,
or when a fairy-tale voice transformed into a
    real-life forehead kiss.

you ever wondered about love's origin, Knucklehead?
about where it all came from?
about the genesis of God's offensive strategy for human survival?
about the divine code for constructing planets that orbit along
    the slanted axes
that keep our stomachs in alignment?
where the butterflies be,
where their plum red, dandelion orange, and cobalt blue wings
be expanding sound waves and restricting the wind's howl.
like, whenever I see him: my man.
you ever loved someone so much it makes your stomach growl?
you ever been both full on—and hungry for—love like *that*?

I FEEL FAMISHED SOMETIMES.

love like *this*
exists in stomach pits full of anxiety about
rejection and abandonment:
a thick and swole lack that makes it hard to swallow and
difficult to digest.
yet, I crave smorgasbords of its sweetness,
and douse it in fear that tastes like acid,
causing love to go down like burnt words mixed in
scorched sugar
that stings the roof of my mouth every time I
breathe and swallow.
sometimes it feels like my throat be full of holes and my belly
be all hollow.

love like *this*
ain't for the queasy.
it ain't for folks who are incapable of keeping heavy things down.
it ain't for folks who can't hold the remainder of their guts together
or for those afraid to dig deep ditches in the shallow ground.
it ain't for those with sensitive tongues either:

picky folks with pompous palates that prefer presentation
over preparation.
it ain't for those who don't believe that practice ain't
about perfection.

love like *this*
is instead for those who desire infinite famine over centuries of
solitude.
for those who'd rather be forever empty than always alone.
it's for those who'd choose to chew and swallow frozen air
rather than gnaw at nothingness wrapped around a hot collarbone.
it's for those who'd bake a billion loaves of faith
before breaking breadcrumbs at a table by themselves.

for real for real, Knucklehead, I think I'd starve without my man,
which ain't as bad as feeling emotionally and physically neglected
by him.
truth is: sometimes we get disconnected.
and it's as if my body ain't attached to my insides anymore,
and so my flesh ain't real enough to desire his imagination like
it used to,
and our mirrors become windows letting all the heat out in
the summer,
but won't shut tight enough to make us warm by winter's
crisp whisper.

and I know why. and it ain't me. it ain't him. it ain't us.

it's the world that don't really love us:
a globe full of gossip that's got us all tangled up and tattered.
got us questioning if our Black gay lives, who we love,
and how we love   matters.
and somehow we get dissolved inside of all that chitchatter,
and wound up taking all that pain and anger out on each other,
pulling all that trauma and sadness and blame from out of each other:
the truth about how we be feeling about all that shit:
the fire. the ash. the gray. the pit.
the space so small only me and my man can fit.

I know we ain't the cause of tension that splits us beneath our ligaments,
between joints, and inside our cartilage and whatnot.
I know we aren't the reason why our arteries, neurons, and tissues tear apart,
and why our words slice, scratch, scrape, and scar.
truth is, Knucklehead, it feels like war.
but me and my man don't do no fistfighting.
nah, he sprouts wings and flies off into space, and I resort to writing.
I be making up metaphors about the gargantuan black anchor

slip-sliding inside out of a blue space, where me and my man be
waist-deep,
swimming on sea waves as if ocean shores don't exist.
for real for real,
I don't think either one of us wanna know how deep all of it can
really get.

and all I know is, it's guaranteed to get darker the farther people
in love
stray away from their natural light.
which means me and my man would dim our shine and disappear
before we could exhale for the last time,
before we wouldn't be able to see each other anymore.
and that just don't feel right.
because I wanna breathe with him forever.

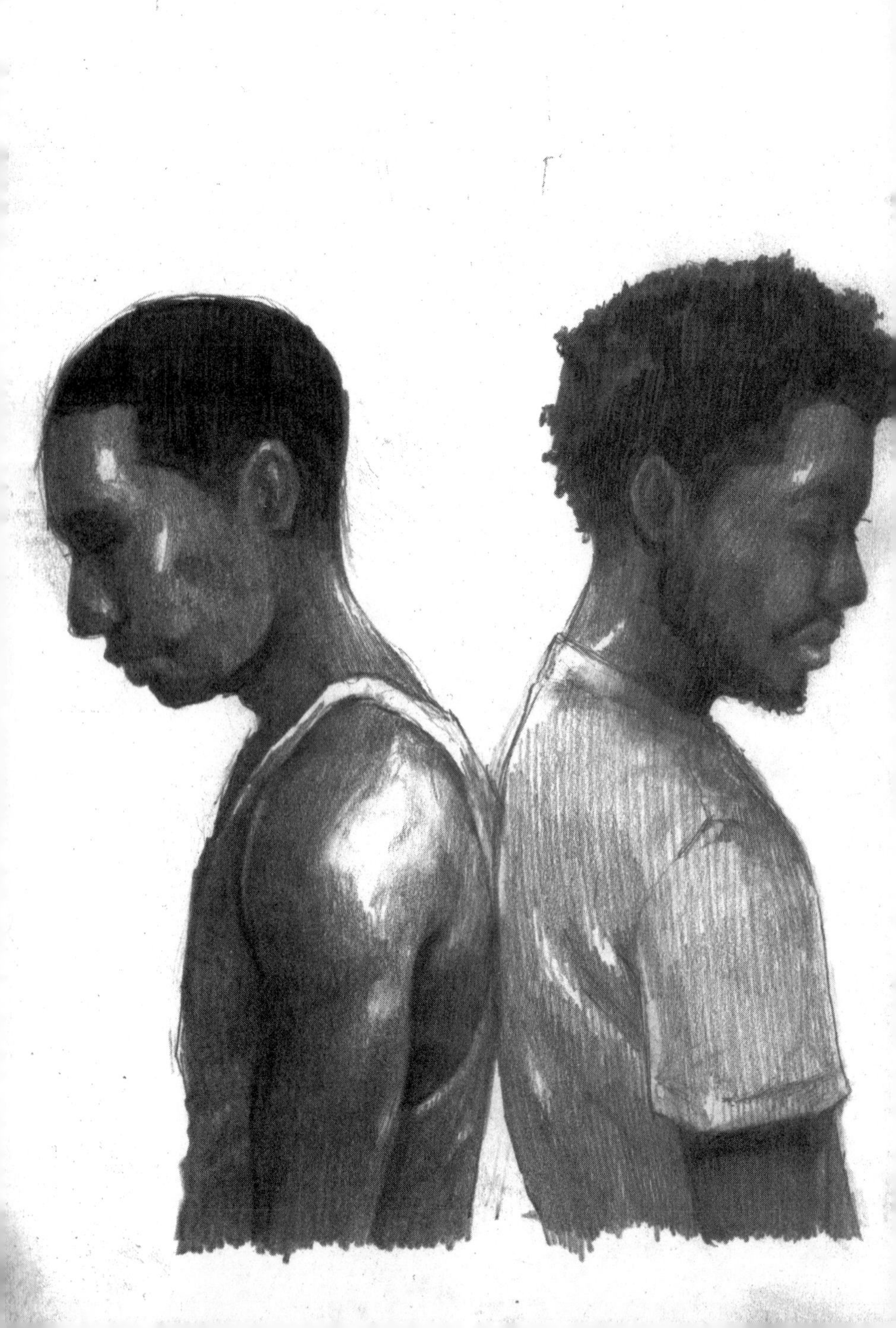

BUT. WHO WE ARE. TOGETHER.

ain't some comic book, fairy tale, reality TV show script.
ain't nothing waiting beyond the credits for us.
ain't no secrets written on cards waiting on cue for us.
ain't no camera capable of capturing how our words fly on the walls
and stick and sting sometimes, and soothe and comfort and heal
and inflate bellies bloated, full of laughter.
ain't no confessional booth safe enough to press play on the bullshit
and still be in love the morning after.

but after every morning, there my man is, with his words:
 inspiring and sharp.
cutting through my tough parts,
exposing where I'm tender
and how I tend to bark at his attempts to be tender;
those moments when I confuse salt with sugar
and taste his words wrong.
I be like, "my bad, my palate is still adjusting to your sweetness."

I'm still discovering how it's possible that saline can be the main
 ingredient

for both blood and love,
and both have to do with a beating heart,
and that a heartbeat can sound like honey but feel like sap.
can't tell if it's the bees or the trees that keep pulling you back.
like a spring. like a swing. like a pendulum.
like a clapper (that thing that makes the Liberty Bell ring).
like a dream.

like figuring it out in front of facing fears. and tears, furious
    and on fire.
flaming f-bombs, smashing egos into pieces,
and then arguing over whose pieces it is.
fussing about what "peace" is.
can't deconstruct conflict in a war zone of masculinity.

two men in love, mad, marking territories, measuring up,
    chests puffed.
pissing contests over misunderstanding context
don't always result in romantic kisses from the movies.
more like fireworks of words on display in the month of December.
got the neighbors scared.
got way too much bass playing upstairs.
all that vibrato rumbling.
meanwhile, two men are fumbling over gender roles,
running crooked on the field, 'cause they ain't straight,
and it ain't that simple.

it's complicated. two men, in love, frustrated.
ain't got nothing to do with who makes dinner,
but has everything to do with what you eat.
ain't got nothing to do with who does the dishes,
it's whether or not they're clean.
simple shit, stored in a bottle of resentment,
which we disguise as clutter kept stashed in the basement . . .

I LOVE HIM LIKE SOUNDS FOUND IN DARK BASEMENTS.

the kind of thud you're scared to face,
a raucous cackle always giving chase that makes you run
and so you run because it feels brave you run because you're
afraid . . .
afraid you'll be pulled back down into a dark familiar space:
some place where monsters have faces and names and no shame

notice that urban legend never ends with the real battle with
the monster: It.
heavy and ugly, breathing on your heels, waiting to see your fear,
waiting for you to fall back down there . . .

no one ever talks about the fight.
no one ever talks about facing demons with bare fist,
no weapons, just knuckles and wrist.
no one talks about the battle.
no one tells you that your skin is not thick enough to withstand
the blows

or that your heart beats harder than your blood can actually flow,
and it makes you feel silly and weak and you can't see . . .

see, no one talks about trying to swing in the darkness.
no flesh tagged, just black monster camouflaged.
It, aiming for your rib cage, and you, just trying to protect your heart.
no one ever talks about it that way.
and yet, somehow, we always manage to make it up the steps,
reach the top, relieved, believed we've dodged death
because instead of weaving right,
we Bob and Steve left and we manage to miss it.

and I almost missed my man
because I ignored the sounds in basements at risk of losing my own life.
and suicide ain't for cowards, Knucklehead,
you gotta be brave enough for *this* fight.
I'm talking bootstraps and booby traps and Grandma's prayers.
you gotta learn to stand at the foot of those stairs
and stare that monster in its eyes
and dare it to move and say, "*love*, I'm not afraid of you."

I DREAMT ABOUT MY MAN.

I had visions about him show up on the page before I knew he existed,
before I felt safe enough to do more than write poetry about his eyes.
I imagined that if I stared at them long enough
I could feel the rhythm in them, and it made my soul start dancing
in random patterns and rhythmic circles
that seemed to spell out letters,
and these letters turned into words,
and these words turned into sentences,
and these sentences turned into poems,
and these poems turned into songs that I liked to sing in the shower.

I liked to watch the words fog up the mirror with their evaporating steam,
and then I'd draw a heart in them,
and it made me feel like we'd just made love.
then I'd take his words and put them into my skin,

get them deep into my pores
only to go out in the hot sun where I start to sweat him.
every single word of my man would begin to trickle down my body
and I'd become a walking dictionary with only definitions of him.

when people looked at me, they'd see him written all over my face
but they couldn't manage to see the word "mine"
that trickled down to my private parts.
and when I was outside, I'd inhale his words and exhale them
into the wind,
and they'd create white sentences inside of a blue sky;
some people called them clouds.
it was funny watching them all try to figure us out,
wondering what those pictures and those symbols could be,
but they didn't realize they were trying to decipher a language:
a communication of love that we got,
and Knucklehead, it ain't that simple.

for what me and my man got is language and communication
that existed before colonization.
we spoke through shadow kisses as our silhouettes
walked along the Serengeti.
we sipped on herbal teas while studying the art of a
Tanzanian sunset.
we lay in the shade drinking lemonade while writing
Swahili poetry.

the kind of poetry I would recite to him on the day of our
    commitment
just so that our ancestors knew I could love my man
    in the "write" way.

now I sit across from him staring at his eyes,
and the history of what we got is written on every single
    strand of his lashes
and when my man blinks, it's like our pages are turning
        like the pages in the books of some of my dreams.

ONE TIME I WROTE A LOVE POEM.

and I read it to myself while I slept.
I kneeled on the floor, closed my eyes, clasped my hands,
and spoke out loud thoughts of me and my love poem
    sleeping together.
I placed pieces of it inside my pen
and wrote it all over the sheets on our bed
and lay in them, and I engulfed myself in the poetry of us.

the words seeped through the sheets and into my skin,
and I absorbed our words and turned them into metaphors
and turned our metaphors into daydreams
and turned our daydreams into nightmares
        where I was running and it was chasing
        and I was falling and it was catching while gravity was
          pulling,
        yet we disappeared before we even hit the ground.

and then I woke up to find myself cuddling up inside
    the letters of us,

curving inside the curves of our words
and smelling the scents made by our sounds.

I wish I didn't have to write cryptic love poems about my man then,
but poetry commanded that I did.
since I couldn't connect to him,
it was the closest way I could have him,
and sometimes I felt like I was beside him
once my pen ground against the paper.
and I had to remember to write at a slow and very steady pace,
keep my words long, big, and deep,
but try not to make them come out too fast,
but Knucklehead,
sometimes it felt so damn good to dot the i's and cross the t's,
I never knew how much longer a love poem would last.
        maybe one two three more stanzas, bars, lines, and
            paragraphs.

and I had to remember to keep a cap on my pen
just to prevent my ink from spilling,
because the next time I wrote about my love poem,
it could've wound up pregnant with twins.
and if it did, we'd just call them baby girl simile and baby boy
  metaphor.

oh, I am so glad I don't have to write love poems like that anymore.

but poetry used to command that I do.
and so every night I would write.
and every night I would dream.
and every night I would wake up
wishing it was its eyes, instead of those words,
and that it was its lips, instead of those verbs,
and that I could kiss it
and swirl my words around in its mouth
and have it chew on my sentences
just so it knew what I was thinking by tasting the flavor
of my prose.

since I couldn't have love realistically
I always had it poetically.

LOVE IS A BALANCING ACT—

a graceful dance between wit and emotion.
a choreographed movement, like waves leaping in oceans.
we all need something . . . a signal that sparks transition.
some reason to change our position. some excuse for shifting.
so on our wedding day, me and my man took the lead
and guided love by the fingertips,
spun it around and around, pulled it closer, and let it drift a bit.
we replicated the same steps and listened for familiar rhythms:
secret melodies inside of songs my man and I hadn't even heard
    or sung yet.

I dreamt that we'd be square-dancing in circles down the aisle,
hoping to catch the beat, hoping for the right time to move our feet,
knowing that we would be giving *the* performance of our lives.
        it would be *a* performance of our lives.
and the whole world would be watching:
an audience of spectators gathered around to watch us
    plié, pirouette,
first position, second position, followed by the third,

then, we'd trip over ourselves
remembering that little Black boys are not supposed to be
ballerinas.

so I dreamt that on our wedding day,
my man and I would dangle masculinity on the tips of our toes.
and I suppose that's the point, right? don't fall.
or if you do, make sure nobody knows.
make sure nobody can question your grace, or your poise,
or your divine capacity to hear instruments, when all others can
hear is noise.
it was *the* performance of our lives
it was *a* performance of our lives.

and my man and I ain't fall. we remained onstage, unafraid,
because the tune we needed finally started to play.
and the musicians and their lyrics and their bass
became sheet music with melodies written all over our faces.
and the singers belted our ballads,
and the two of us danced,
never dropping hands from night until noon.

and the day after, my man and I took a sweet flight for our
honeymoon.

WE MADE IT: LOVE.

I watched my husband sleep,
his head against the airplane window
I was thinking how some folks ain't know Black boys could float
    up here
like *that*, where we were: us, flying inside the blue sky,
flapping only our softest feathers,
blowing kisses in between clouds,
causing the wind to bounce us all around
as if everything is meant to be buoyant up there, where we were . . .

        where our breath became verses written into the breeze
        and so, we hang glided across the tops of tall trees,
        suspending ourselves high above the bottom of
            sturdy bridges
        that were built on nothing but trust and faith alone.

we were together up there   where we were . . .
        where gravity kept pulling us into our centers
        causing our cores to warm and our middles to melt,

and we were just Black skin, hot, smooth, and strong with
nails and fingers
and toes and wrinkles on hands
symmetrical to lines spread across our thick foreheads,
where we both be black marrow,
deep, sweat-soaked, shined up, and stashed inside trenches
burrowed inside our bones,
where it just be dark berry, very sweet juice.

some folks ain't know we could squeeze within ourselves like *that*,
all while holding on to each other,   up there,   where we were
us, overlapping into one another,
folding underneath brown flesh,
peeling back and pulling up the private parts of us
that keep our entire Black bodies whole
and that make our knuckles swell as if sucking in too
much sugar
and spitting out something divine.

and Knucklehead, my husband is fine.
so I enjoyed watching his eyes roll back and forth,
wondering what he was dreaming about
and whether he too was writing a poem.

DEAR KNUCKLEHEAD,

I was a poet who was afraid to publish.
I was worried about seeing my words printed in a book,
and a back cover would be all these blurbs like,
    "this is a national bestseller,"
"a must-read," "what a wonderful account of an artist's words."
I think it's absurd, for some, to only use their art for profit.
and I'm not trying to justify the lifestyle of a starving artist,
but I feel like if art really is your gift,
then starving at some point should be a part of it.
I feel like there should be some pangs in the pit of your stomach
when your notebooks are empty, and ain't no more
    ink left in your pen,
when you aren't changing lives, and your paper is thin.

I've accepted that at some point my economic reality
may rely on my poetic balladry,
and I'm not sure my poems are as good as I think they are,
but I know that I am no longer willing to sell my soul
just to write some fallacies.

and Knucklehead, I have.
I've written wedding poems and birthday poems
and poems about anniversaries,
and poems that spice up *other people's* love lives,
and sometimes I feel dirty and used and confused about
whether or not they actually heard me.
sometimes I wish I could turn the volume down on my words
and transform my performances into conversations
where I can just be Tony Keith Jr.: the poet, the educator, and
the nerd.

for real for real, I wanna be known as that artsy-fartsy intellect
who believed that there is power in his words.
and that I not only took responsibility for what I said,
but was accountable to those who heard,
whether or not I pissed them off
or convinced them to change the world.

look, Knucklehead, sometimes I got tired
and sometimes I got weary,
but I kept on writing even when my vision was blurry,
even when I couldn't see right in front of me,
even when my wrist buckled under the pressure from writing
with fury,
even when people told me I needed to "sit still."
they'd say, "boy, grass never grows under your feet."

I'd say, "Ma, Pop, Grandma, that's because I'm way too busy
climbing uphill."
I'd tell them I don't have time to rest
until the rest of my poems are written.
but I can't stop writing, so none of my poems have endings.
just transitions between new beginnings
and space savers, while refilling the ink in my pen again,
or moments when I need to stop, sleep, and dream
just to recharge my system,
or moments when I need to set my pen on record and just listen . . .

listen, I'm trying to think of myself through a literary breakthrough.
break down walls of bondage with poetic correspondence.
and when I have to make other people feel uncomfortable.
make their spirits feel unsettled,
while my feet keep pushing on these pedals,
'cause I've got no choice but to keep pushing through.

Knucklehead, I'm doing what I'm called to do,
and if you're open to receiving, then the next call might be for you,
and if you don't answer, don't worry,
I've got enough agency and I can collect when the payment is due.
granted, I've got more than a couple of degrees,
and my bank account probably won't go completely in the red
if I spent a couple of pennies,
but I've only got two cents to my name,

and the life that I'm trying to live actually requires change,
    but I've got bills,
so I guess I'm gonna have to keep on writing until
my soul gets saturated and my wallet gets filled.

some people say, "Tony, don't worry, it's faith that will
    get you through."
and I say, "well, if that's the case, then faith,
    I invoke you as my muse!
faith, I invoke you as my power of attorney!
faith, I want you to take over for me, when I can't
    take over for myself.
faith, I want you to take over for me
        when my ego can no longer control my wealth.
faith, I don't want you to be afraid to pull the plug
    from my microphones
        and wipe all my notebooks off the shelf.
faith, I don't want you to be afraid to let me flatline,
        let me lie there until my heart gets back to beating at a
            humble grind.
                resuscitate the power of God back into my lungs
                and let me create new poems, pure and simple
                    ones:
poems about failure and poems about victory,
poems that rhyme occasionally,
poems that resist artistic prisons,

poems that break the chains of writer's block,
and poems that enforce how a pen can be a lethal system."

Knucklehead, I was a poet who was afraid to publish,
until I learned to publish on stages,
where I earned an honest living on free open mic wages.

ACKNOWLEDGMENTS

Thanks, Ma, for letting me write poems as a kid while most boys played sports.

Thanks, Pop, for your endless supply of positive affirmations.

Thank you, Toby and Crystal, for always reminding me to look into my poems for the source.

A special thanks to the dope Black boys with Youth Guidance DC's BAM-FI for inspiring so many parts of this project!